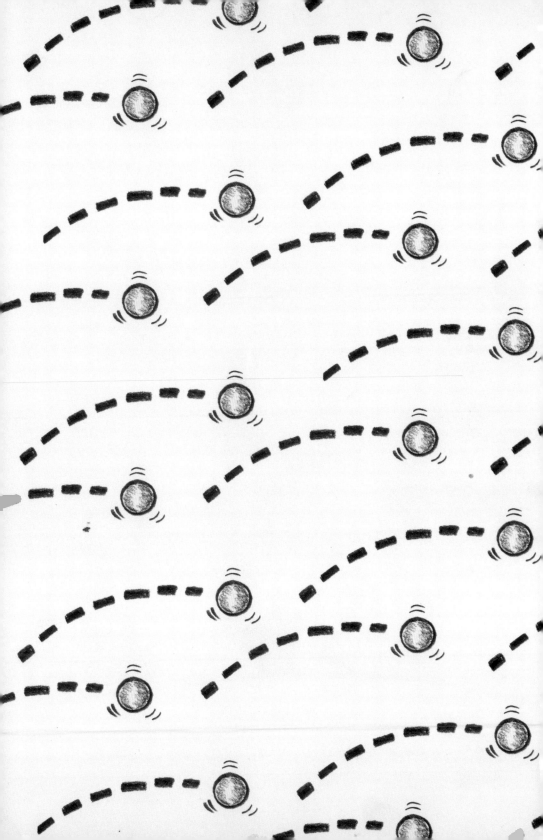

To Zat and Nellie
for playing along

Text and illustrations copyright © 2010 by Mo Willems

Printed in Malaysia
Reinforced binding

First Edition, June 2010
20 19 18 17 16 15 14 13 12 11 10
FAC-029191-15268
Library of Congress Cataloging-in-Publication Data on file.
ISBN 978-1-4231-1991-3
Visit www.hyperionbooksforchildren.com and www.pigeonpresents.com

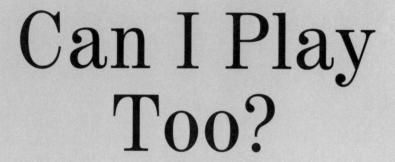

Can I Play Too?

By Mo Willems

An ELEPHANT & PIGGIE Book

Hyperion Books for Children / *New York*

AN IMPRINT OF DISNEY BOOK GROUP

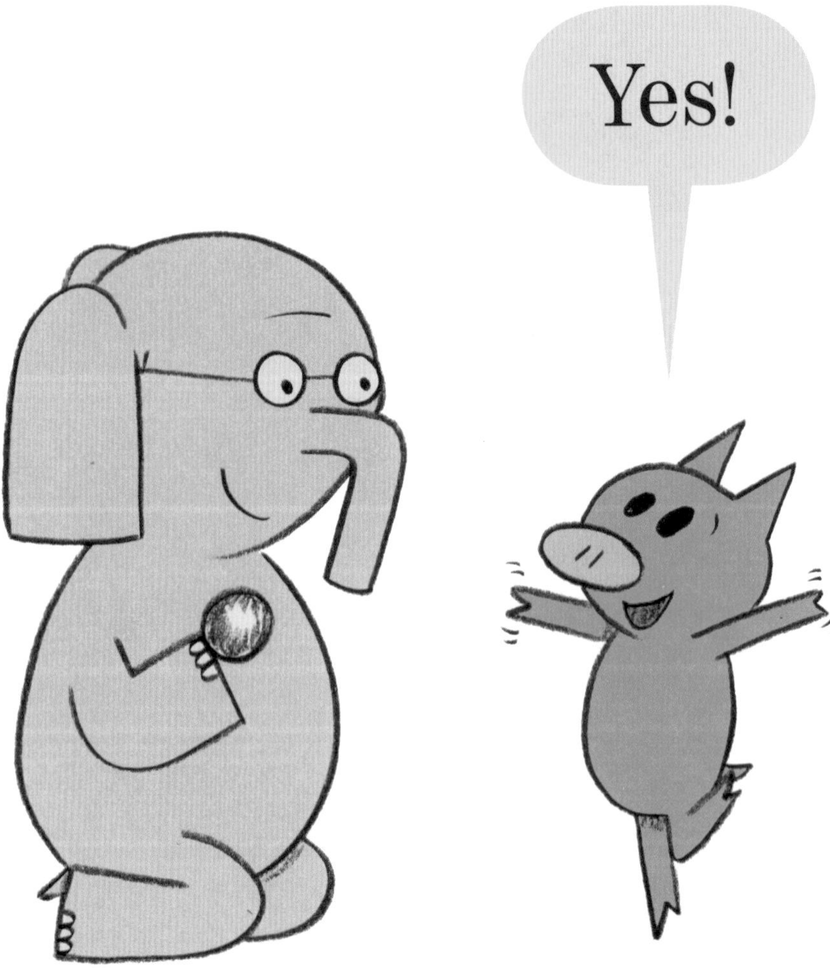
Yes!

I will catch!

8

Can I play too?

We are playing catch.

15

17

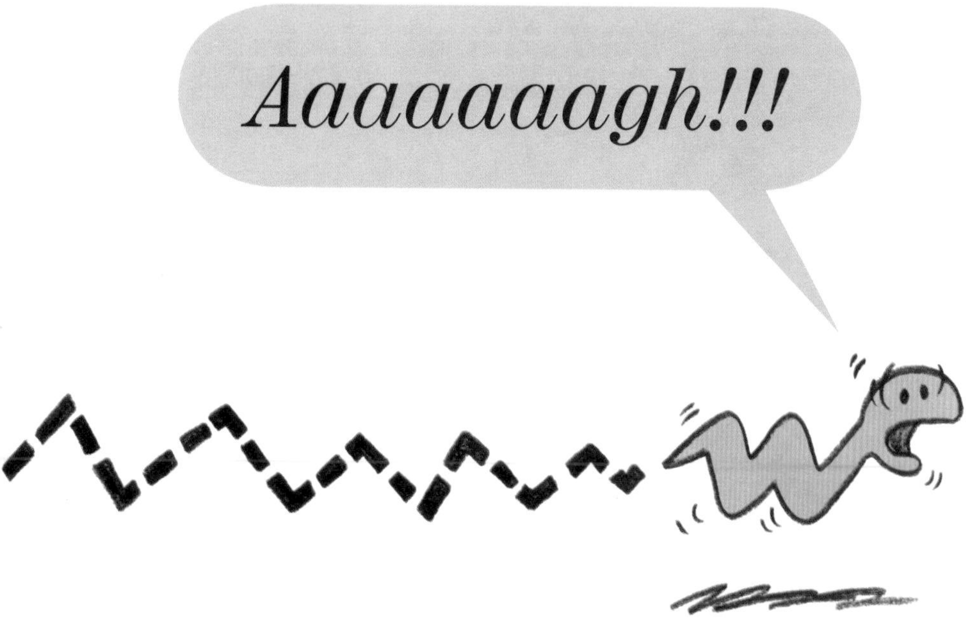
Aaaaaaaagh!!!

23

26

But I can *try*.

29

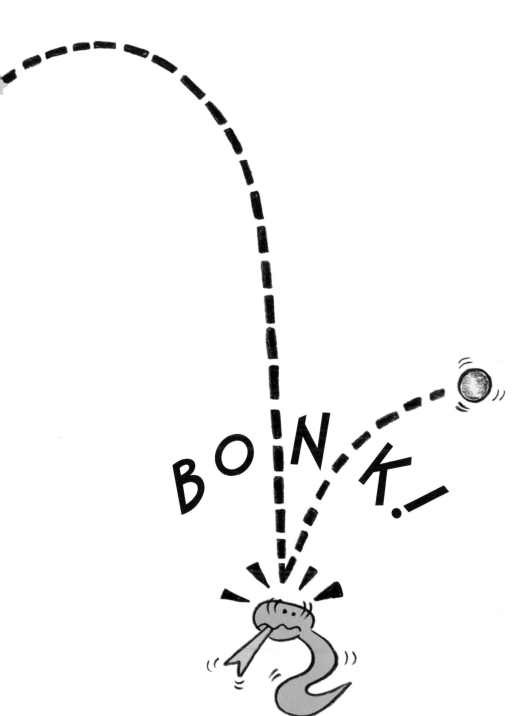

BONK!

It is
okay.

Let's try
again.

33

BONK!

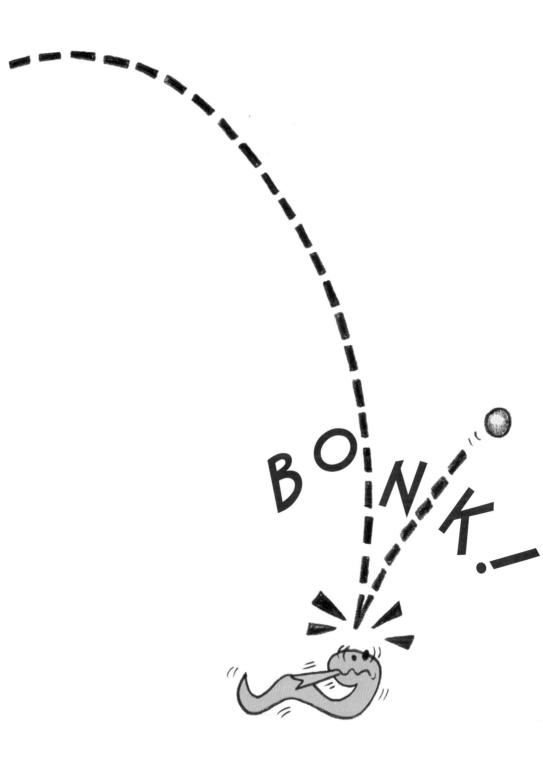

37

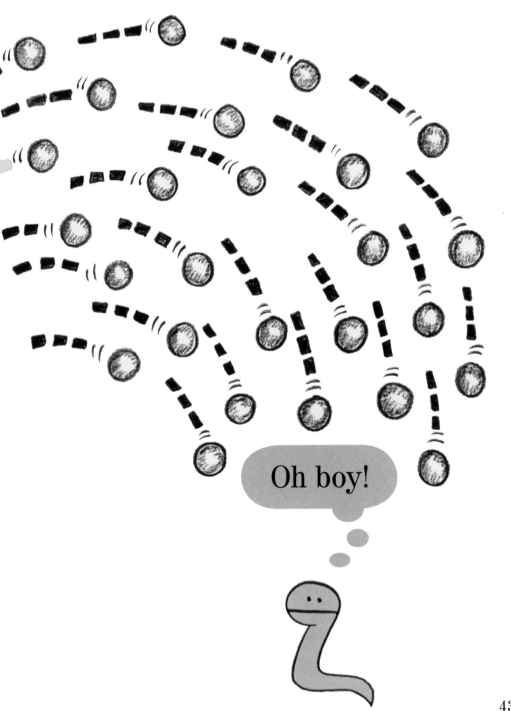

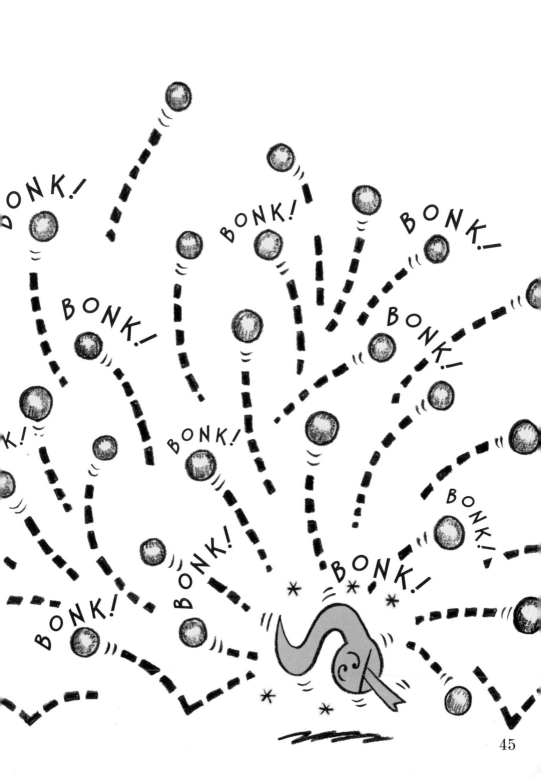

45

WAIT!

49

51

53

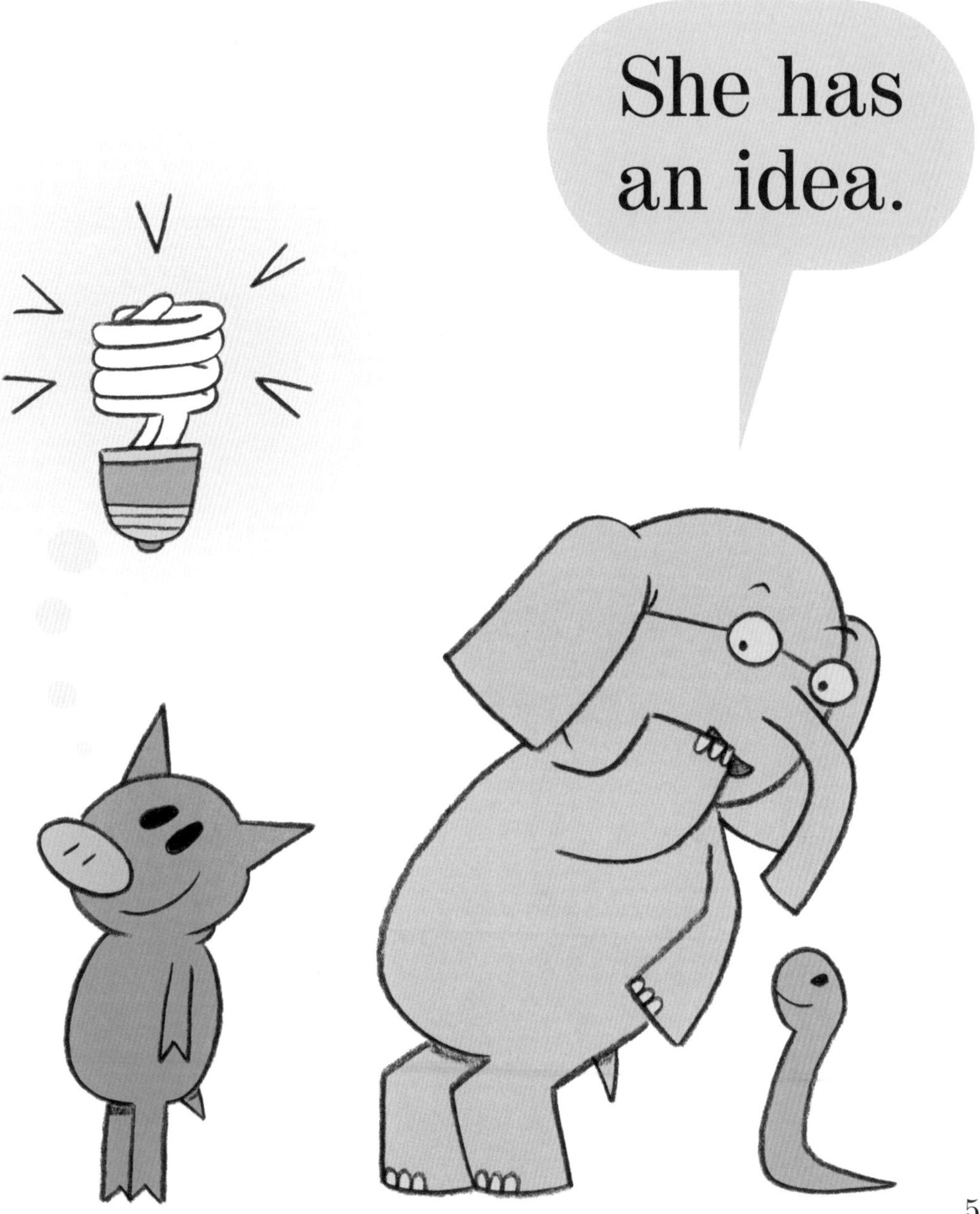
She has
an idea.

Elephant and Piggie have more funny adventures in: